DANGER RANGERS®

BLAZIN' HOT

Written by D. A. Caruso
Edited by Jerry Houser

Art Direction by Susan Sullivan
Illustrated by Louis Scarborough, Ron LaChance, and John Ott
Revised and designed by Rocky Hill Group and Judy O Productions, Inc.

Educational Adventures is proud to say that this book has been approved as an excellent read-aloud storybook for young children by a leading national literacy and reading expert. Professor Linda B. Gambrell of the Eugene T. Moore School of Education at Clemson University is an author and expert in the field of reading. Among Professor Gambrell's many distinctions, she is past president of the National Reading Conference, College Reading Association and she was recently elected to serve as president of the International Reading Association.

The Danger Rangers® is the exclusive property of

www.e3a.com

Dear Parents,

In dangerous emergencies, children need to know what they can do to keep themselves, their families, and their communities safe. This story shows what children can do when they discover a burning house.

First, they must be told how to get help and second they must learn fire safety rules to protect themselves and others.

The Danger Rangers, an adventurous team of lovable characters, lead the way in providing the safety tips. Valuable lessons are learned about what to do when a blaze occurs in your home or neighborhood. Fortunately, no one gets harmed in this story—the Danger Rangers and firefighters save the day.

No one wants a fire to endanger her own life or the lives of others; taking steps to prevent fires in the first place is crucial. The most important step is to adhere to strict rules about children playing with matches, fire setting, and other activities that increase the risk of fire. Conversations about how to avoid fires should be held with the entire family. To take every precaution, home safety checks should be performed and a fire escape plan should be in place.

In a real emergency, remember this Danger Rangers story about how to get help and stay safe.

—Alvin F. Poussaint, M.D.

Dr. Poussaint is Professor of Psychiatry at Harvard Medical School and the Judge Baker Children's Center in Boston.

Born and raised in East Harlem in a family of eight children, Dr. Poussaint graduated from Columbia and received his MD from Cornell. He then took postgraduate training at UCLA Neuropsychiatric Institute, where he served as Chief Resident in Psychiatry.

Dr. Poussaint served as a script consultant to NBC's The Cosby Show *and continues to consult to the media as an advocate of more responsible programming. He is a regular consultant for children's books, television shows, and movies.*

Squeeky   Burt

Sully   Burble

Gabriela

Kitty

Meet the

These six brave superheroes of safety are out to make the world a safer place by eliminating one danger at a time. From their top-secret headquarters deep inside Mount Rushmore, the Danger Rangers are ready to leap into action at a moment's notice!

SULLY is the leader and spokes-seal. He's safety-driven, smart, and funny.

KITTY is cool, smart, and adventurous; the brains of the team.

BURBLE is the team's heart and soul, the power-house and practical joker.

BURT is the very creative and part genius Personal Safety expert.

GABRIELA is the highly skilled Chief of Operations and head safety trainer.

SQUEEKY may be the smallest Danger Ranger but he's also the loudest. Good things come in small packages.

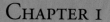

CHAPTER 1

Skateboard Buddies

Ricky Masker and Harry Hopper zigzagged through the park on their skateboards. They were best friends and did everything together—everything except for one thing. Last summer, Ricky became a Junior Danger Ranger.

"What do you want to do this summer?" asked Ricky. They leaned to the right and zoomed down the path.

"Maybe I could be a Junior Danger Ranger like you!" said Harry.

"You have to learn all of the safety rules," said Ricky. "And the first thing you need to remember is to always **BE ALERT**."

"How do I do that?" Harry asked.

"Keep your eyes open and know what's going on around you." Ricky looked behind them. "See little Sally over there?"

"I see her," said Harry. "She's playing."

"What else do you see?"

"She's bouncing a ball."

"And?" asked Ricky.

Harry looked at Sally again. Then he saw it. "Her shoe! Her shoe lace is untied!" he cried.

"Way to go!" said Ricky.

Ricky and Harry helped Sally tie her shoe.

Sally saw the **S**afety **A**lert **V**ect**O**meter (**SAVO**) unit on Ricky's wrist. "Thank you, Junior Danger Ranger," she said.

"You should always make sure your shoe laces are tied, so you don't trip or get them caught on anything," Ricky reminded her.

Mission complete, Ricky and Harry zoomed off on their skateboards.

"That was so cool!" said Harry. "I can't wait to become a Junior Danger Ranger."

CHAPTER 2

House on Fire!

Ricky and Harry zipped down the street and around the corner. Suddenly something caught Ricky's eye and he came to a screeching halt.

"Look! My house!" cried Ricky. "My house is on fire!"

Fear swept over Harry. "What do we do?" he asked.

"**STAY CALM**," said Ricky, remembering his Junior Danger Ranger training. "I need you to go to my neighbor, Mrs. Waters. Tell her there's a fire at my house and that you need to call 911. Then make sure you give them your name and the address of my house. Let them know that it's on fire and someone might be inside."

Tell 911 your name and your address. Tell them there is a fire and if someone is in the building.

"Don't worry, Ricky," said Harry. "I can do this."

Putting their hands together, they both shouted the Danger Ranger motto, "Safety Rules!"

Harry zoomed to Mrs. Waters' house, leaving Ricky all alone.

Ricky sat down on his skateboard. He called into his Junior Danger Ranger Safety Alert Vectometer, "SAVO, there's a fire at 4 Woodburn Lane! Come quickly! I think my father and sister might be in the house."

Ricky wanted to run inside, but he knew **NOT** to enter the burning house—the best thing to do was wait for the firefighters to come.

Never go into a burning building, even if it's your own house. It's very, very dangerous.

CHAPTER 3

Ready for Danger, Rangers!

"Calling all Danger Rangers!" announced SAVO, the Safety Alert Vectometer. His computer voice boomed over the loudspeakers deep inside the secret headquarters in Mount Rushmore. **"DANGER ALERT! DANGER ALERT!"**

His lights flashed and blinked as he beeped louder and louder.

"Calling all Danger Rangers! Report for duty!"

Immediately the Danger Rangers rushed to their waiting hovercraft.

"Looks like one of our Junior Danger Rangers needs our help," said Sully pointing out Ricky on one of the hovercraft's big video screens.

"Right you are, Sully," said SAVO. "Ricky's house is on fire and his father and sister are still inside."

"We need to get there and get them out fast. That fire is spreading quickly," added Squeeky.

SAVO scanned the hovercraft for a final check. "We have no time to lose, Danger Rangers. Prepare for takeoff!" boomed SAVO. As they buckled up, the engines roared and everyone shouted the Danger Ranger motto, "Safety Rules!"

Without a second to lose, the hovercraft blasted out of George Washington's mouth and the Danger Rangers were on their way.

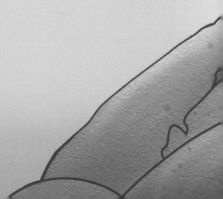

CHAPTER 4

No Time to Lose!

As soon as the hovercraft landed, the Danger Rangers quickly jumped out.

"Am I glad to see you, Danger Rangers!" said Ricky, as he ran up to meet them. "I sent my friend Harry to dial 911 and I didn't let anyone go inside the house."

"Good job, Ricky," said Sully, "When there's fire about—
STAY OUT!"

"And don't you worry," Burt added, "We'll get your father and sister out safe and sound."

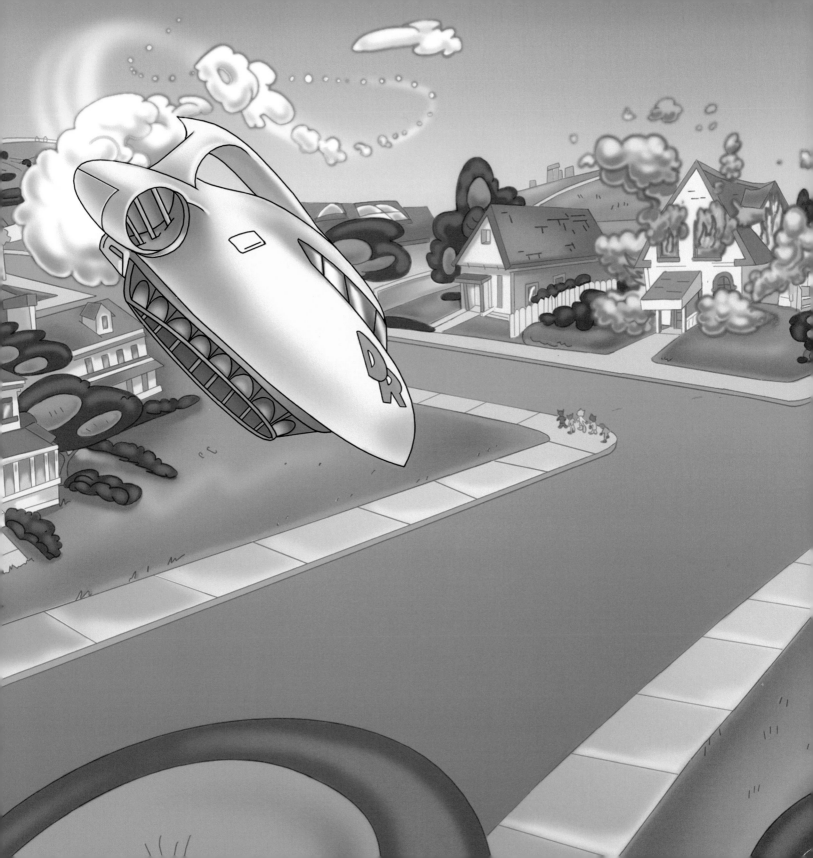

Chapter 5

Hello? Anyone Here?

If you're stuck in a room and can't get out right away, lay wet cloths at the bottom of doors to stop the smoke from coming under them.

"It's really hard to see in here," said Kitty, as she tried to find her way through the smoke in the burning house.

"Breathing *smoke* is really dangerous!" yelled Sully.

"I'm on it. We need to keep the smoke out," responded Kitty.

She crawled along the floor and found her way to the kitchen. There, she wet a bunch of towels and put them along the bottom of the doors to keep the smoke out.

Meanwhile, Sully crawled through the living room, yelling all the while,
"Hello? Is anyone here?"

Finally he heard a loud cough. Pointing his Safety Alert Vectometer unit in
the direction of the cough, Sully found Mr. Masker. He was lying on the floor in
the hallway.

"I can't find my daughter, my little Rosie!" Mr. Masker coughed.

"Follow me," said Sully.

"And stay low, under the smoke," said Burt. "Smoke rises, so the best air will be near the floor."

"Did you and your family have a fire escape plan?" asked Sully.

"No, we didn't. We meant to do it, but we never did," said Mr. Masker.

"Where was Rosie the last time you saw her?" asked Sully.

"I can't remember," Mr. Masker coughed again. "You have to find her. Please!"

Always stay low to the floor, under the smoke. It's easier to breathe and you won't hurt your lungs.

CHAPTER 6

Search and Rescue

"Hey, I've been lookin' all over for you guys," said Squeeky.

"We have to find Rosie," said Sully. "She's missing."

Kitty and Burble shouted from the kitchen, "We'll look in here." The smoke was still thick but the wet towels had stopped it from seeping in from under the door.

"Good teamwork, Rangers!" said Sully, "Burt, see if you can get down those hallways. Squeeky, you stay with me."

Sully pointed down another hallway. "Mr. Masker, where does this hallway lead?"

"The playroom," said Mr. Masker. "Maybe Rosie's in there!" Panicking a bit, he started to run to the door.

"Not so fast!" said Squeeky, stopping him. "*Even in an emergency you gotta try to stay calm so you can think straight.*"

"Hey, guys," said Sully, in a low voice. "I see something!" Sully pointed into the living room. A fluffy tail was sticking out from behind the chair. "Rosie . . . Rosie?" called Sully, but she didn't respond.

"If that's her hiding behind the chair, she must be really scared," said Squeeky.

Sully motioned to Squeeky to go behind the chair.

When inside, never hide. The firefighters are your friends.

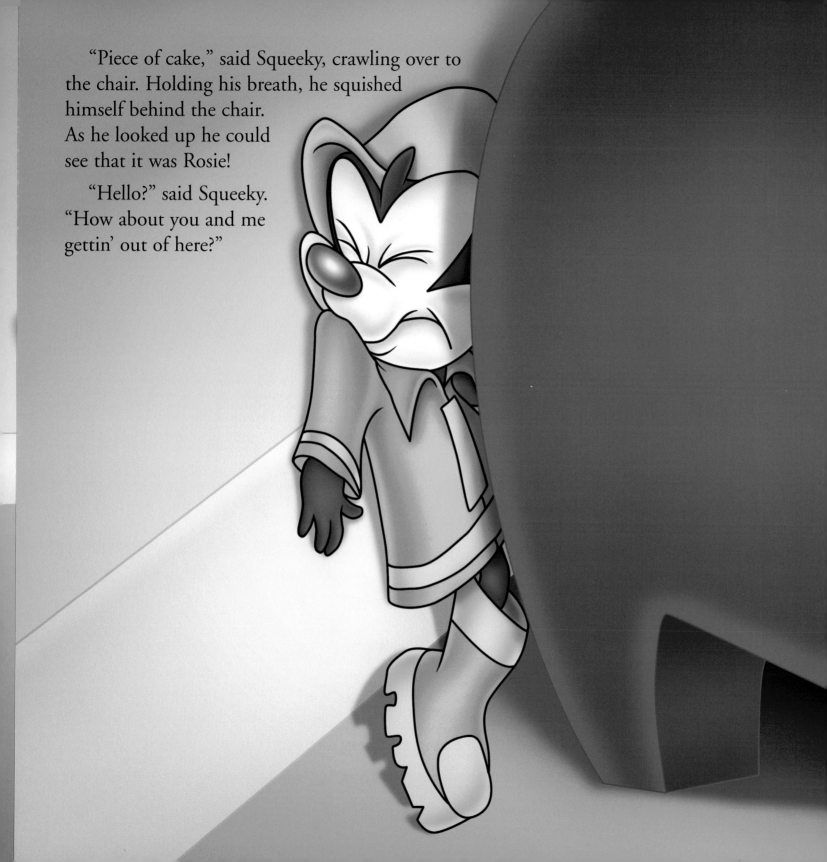

"Piece of cake," said Squeeky, crawling over to the chair. Holding his breath, he squished himself behind the chair. As he looked up he could see that it was Rosie!

"Hello?" said Squeeky. "How about you and me gettin' out of here?"

CHAPTER 7
Don't Open that Door!

Never open a door in a burning house. Carefully and gently check first to see if it's hot. You never know if there's a fire behind it.

Immediately Burt pulled his arms and legs into his shell and made himself into a ball. Sully rolled him across the room and Burt landed right in front of Rosie, just in time to stop her. He popped out of his shell. "Don't open that door!" he warned.

"But my Silly Milly doll is in there!" said Rosie.

Sully rushed up. "Don't ever open a door without checking it first," he added. "You never know if there's a fire behind it."

Your life is more valuable than anything else. Don't stay inside to look for your favorite things. Get out! Meet your family outside!

Sully carefully and gently touched the closed door. "*Ouch*! That's hot all right!"

"We can't open it!" shouted Burt "It's hot because there's a fire on the other side!"

"But I need Silly Milly." Rosie had tears in her eyes. "She's my best friend."

Kitty crawled over to Rosie. "Rosie, I know you love your Silly Milly," said Kitty. "But you have to remember that you are more important than anything else–even your favorite doll."

CHAPTER 8

Danger Rangers Save the Day!

Vroom! Vroom! The fire trucks zoomed down the street and stopped in front of the burning house. The firefighters jumped out and hooked up their hoses as Ricky told them everything he knew about the situation.

Suddenly, the front door to the burning house swung open.

Ricky and Harry looked up and watched Sully run out of the house. He was carrying Rosie in his arms.

Then the rest of the Danger Rangers came out with Burble carrying Mr. Masker.

Ricky ran up and gave Rosie and his father great big hugs.

"I'm very proud of you, Ricky," said Mr. Masker. "You helped save our lives."

"Thank you, Ricky," said Rosie.

"And thank *you*, Danger Rangers," said Mr. Masker.

Off to the side, Harry looked down at the sidewalk. He kicked a rock. Everyone was too busy to pay any attention to him.

"I'll never become a Junior Danger Ranger," he sighed.

CHAPTER 9

Harry Becomes a Junior Danger Ranger!

Everyone watched from a safe distance as the firefighters worked to put out the fire. Everyone, that is, except Harry.

"Harry Hopper?" asked Sully.

Harry looked up. "Wow, Ranger Sully!"

"We've been watching you, Harry," said Sully.

"And we're proud of what you did today," said Kitty.

"You are?" asked Harry.

"You helped Ricky in an emergency and ran to his neighbor's house to dial 911," said Sully. "So today, we'd like to make you an official Junior Danger Ranger."

Sully slapped the Safety Alert Vectometer unit onto Harry's wrist.

"This is so cool!" Harry smiled.

"Way cool!" said Ricky.

"Now you are both Junior Danger Rangers," Squeeky said proudly.

"You know what this means, guys?" asked Burt. "Now you have an important job to do this summer."

"I'm ready!" said Harry.

"Danger Ranger Ready," said Ricky.

"We want you to be on the alert and on the lookout for dangers, wherever they may be," said Burble.

They both promised to be on Danger Alert and call SAVO whenever they needed their help. Then the Danger Rangers all gave the boys a big thumbs up and smile.

"Have a safe summer!" the Danger Rangers called out, as they boarded their hovercraft. The engines fired up and roared as it lifted off the ground. It shot up and into the sky and disappeared into the clouds.

CHAPTER 10

Fire Safety Rules!

Back at Danger Ranger headquarters, Sully and the gang were all gathered in the debriefing room.

"Job well done, Danger Rangers," said SAVO.

"This case, Blazin' Hot, really showed us how important it is to know the fire safety rules," said Sully. "It's sure good to know that Ricky and Harry are Danger Ranger Ready."

"I sleep better knowing there are more kids out there who know our motto," added SAVO.

"Safety Rules!" the Danger Rangers all shouted.

Kitty pulled out her notebook and wrote down the . . .

Fire Safety Rules

1. In case of a fire or any other emergency, dial 911.
2. Tell 911 your name and your address. Tell them there is a fire and if someone is in the building.
3. Never go into a burning building, even if it's your own house. It's very, very dangerous.
4. When inside, never hide. The firefighters are your friends.
5. Your life is more valuable than anything else. Don't stay inside to look for your favorite things. Get out! Meet your family outside!
6. Never open a door in a burning house. Carefully and gently check first to see if it's hot. You never know if there's a fire behind it.
7. Always stay low to the floor, under the smoke. It's easier to breathe and you won't hurt your lungs.
8. If you're stuck in a room and can't get out right away, lay wet cloths at the bottom of doors to stop the smoke from coming under them.
9. Make sure your family has a fire escape plan!

Kitty closed her notebook. "OK guys, this case is officially wrapped up," said Kitty.

Safety Rules!